THE BANK STREET
CREEPY TALES

GRAPHIC STORY COMICS ADAPTING THE WORK OF
EDGAR ALLAN POE AND JACK LONDON
AND OTHER WORLD-FAMOUS AUTHORS OF CHILLING TALES

Edited by Howard Zimmerman,
Seymour Reit, and Barbara Brenner

A Byron Preiss Book

POCKET BOOKS

New York   London   Toronto   Sydney   Tokyo

ACKNOWLEDGMENTS

This collection was in every sense a team effort. The editors would like to thank the following people for their contribution to this unique series:

At Bank Street College of Education

Jim Levine, William Hooks, Barbara Brenner, Seymour Reit, Linda Greengrass, Virginia Kwarta, Sam Brian, Lorenzo Martinez and Margaret Peet.

At Byron Preiss Visual Publications, Inc.

Howard Zimmerman, Mary Higgins, Gwendolyn Smith, David Keller, and Ruth Ashby.

At Simon & Schuster

Patricia MacDonald, Jonathon Brodman, Pat Cool, Joanne Goodman, and Mary Frundt.

And finally, our thanks to those authors whose works have been adapted for this series, and to those artists and writers who brought the stories to life.

LEVITATION Copyright © 1989 by Joseph Payne Brennan. JIMMY TAKES VANISHING LESSONS Copyright © 1959 by Walter R. Brooks. Copyright © renewal 1987 by Dorothy Brooks. SUBWAY Copyright © 1989 by Byron Preiss Visual Publications, Inc.

Mechanicals by Mary Griffin
Book lettered by Gary Fields

This novel is a work of fiction. Names, characters, places and incidents are either the product of the author's imagination or are used fictitiously. Any resemblance to actual events or locales or persons, living or dead, is entirely coincidental.

Another *Original* publication of POCKET BOOKS

POCKET BOOKS, a division of Simon & Schuster Inc.
1230 Avenue of the Americas, New York, NY 10020

Copyright © 1989 by Byron Preiss Visual Publications, Inc.
Introduction copyright © 1989 by Bank Street College
Cover artwork copyright © 1989 by Byron Preiss Visual Publications, Inc.

All rights reserved, including the right to reproduce this book or portions thereof in any form whatsoever. For information address Pocket Books, 1230 Avenue of the Americas, New York, NY 10020

ISBN: 0-671-63147-0

First Pocket Books trade paperback printing September 1989

10 9 8 7 6 5 4 3 2 1

POCKET and colophon are registered trademarks of Simon & Schuster, Inc.

Printed in U.S.A.

Contents

A Message from Bank Street

Many famous writers have written ghost stories and other forms of the creepy tale. In Shakespeare's play, *Hamlet,* for instance, the Prince of Denmark meets the ghost of his father. This meeting sparks the action of the whole drama—but creepy tales go back long before Shakespeare's time.

Some people say that the first scary stories were told to help people explain the great mysteries that they didn't understand—like death. Whatever the reason, great writers down through the ages seem to have been drawn to write on themes that send shivers up people's backs.

In creepy stories, ghosts usually are the spirits of dead people, but there are "non-human" ghosts as well. The legend of the Flying Dutchman is about a haunted ship. A famous movie, *The Red Shoes,* tells of a "possessed" pair of ballet slippers.

Before the 1800s creepy tales dealt mostly with "actual" spirits supposedly seen by real people. During those years, especially in England, there were many reports of ghostly figures flitting about in old castles, graveyards and haunted houses. Then later on, writers began dreaming up their *own* supernatural figures. The great Charles Dickens was one of the leaders of this trend. Everyone knows his fable, *A Christmas Carol,* in which various ghosts come to plague the miser Ebenezer Scrooge.

In America the first important creepy tale may have been *The Legend of Sleepy Hollow* by Washington Irving, which appeared in 1820. Then came the stories of Edgar Allan Poe. In the 1830s Poe wrote a collection of weird stories called *Tales of the Grotesque.* Since then numerous authors have used creepy themes—among them Oscar Wilde, Mary Shelley, Thomas Mann, H. P. Lovecraft, Agatha Christie and Ray Bradbury.

Most ghosts in literature are frightening critters. But not all of them. Sometimes ''creeps'' can be funny, as in *The Water Ghost of Harrowby Hall,* which you'll find in this book. You'll also find many other interesting spooks in these ''haunted'' pages.

Why do people enjoy reading creepy tales or seeing them in the movies and on TV? Nobody knows for sure. Maybe they're popular because our imaginations are stimulated by the weird and supernatural. Let's face it—at times, there's nothing like a good scare!

LEVITATION
BY
JOSEPH PAYNE BRENNAN

Story Adapted by Howard Zimmerman

Illustrated by Lee Moyer

MORGAN'S WONDER CARNIVAL MOVED INTO RIVERVILLE FOR A ONE-NIGHT SHOW.

MORGAN'S WASN'T A LARGE CARNIVAL, BUT IT WAS THE ONLY SHOW AROUND. THE CLOSEST MOVIE THEATER TO RIVERVILLE WAS 90 MILES AWAY.

THE PEOPLE OF RIVERVILLE ENJOYED THE CARNIVAL. THEY CRAMMED PEANUTS AND POPCORN INTO THEIR MOUTHS, AND DRANK CUP AFTER CUP OF PINK LEMONADE.

STEP RIGHT UP, LADIES AND GENTLEMEN! HONDU WILL ASTOUND AND AMAZE YOU-- WITH IMPOSSIBLE FEATS OF MAGIC AND MYSTERY!

THE CROWD GREW QUIET. HONDU'S DARK EYES MOVED QUICKLY FROM SIDE TO SIDE, MISSING NOTHING.

I WILL NEED A VOLUNTEER FOR MY DEMONSTRATION. IF SOMEONE FROM AMONG YOU WILL KINDLY STEP FORWARD--

THE CROWD LOOKED UP... BUT NOBODY MOVED.

I CANNOT PERFORM UNLESS SOMEONE COMES UP. I ASSURE YOU, THERE IS NO DANGER.

9

10

THE CROWD WAS SILENT. FINALLY, HONDU CALMED DOWN ENOUGH TO CONTINUE.

FOR THE SHOW TO CONTINUE, I WILL NEED A NEW VOLUNTEER.

PERHAPS THE PERSON WHO THREW THE POPCORN WOULD CARE TO COME UP? OR IS HE AFRAID?

FRANK DIDN'T LIKE BEING CALLED A COWARD. HE DECIDED TO GO UP ONSTAGE... AND RUIN THE SHOW.

AT FIRST, FRANK RESISTED HONDU'S COMMAND TO RELAX. BUT SOON HIS ANGER DISAPPEARED... AND HE OBEYED.

HONDU COMMANDED THAT FRANK LIE DOWN ON THE PLATFORM.

YOU ARE FALLING ASLEEP... YOU **ARE** ASLEEP. YOU WILL DO ANYTHING I TELL YOU TO... ANYTHING.

SUDDENLY, A NEW NOTE ENTERED HONDU'S VOICE. THE AUDIENCE BECAME TENSE.

I COMMAND YOU TO RISE FROM THE PLATFORM. DO NOT STAND UP-- BUT RISE FROM THE PLATFORM!

RISE! I COMMAND YOU-- RISE!

13

FRANK DID NOT STOP. HE CONTINUED TO RISE INTO THE AIR WITHOUT ANY AID OR SUPPORT.

SUDDENLY, THE HYPNOTIST CRUMPLED TO THE PLATFORM. THERE WERE CALLS FOR A DOCTOR...

THE BARKER RAN OVER... BUT HONDU WAS ALREADY BEYOND HELP.

HE'S DEAD. MUST HAVE BEEN HIS HEART.

JUST THEN, A WOMAN IN THE CROWD SCREAMED.

14

EVEN AFTER HONDU'S DEATH, FRANK CONTINUED TO OBEY HIS FINAL COMMAND: "RISE!"

COME DOWN, FRANK! COME DOWN!

WAKE UP, FRANK! STOP! COME DOWN!

BUT THE RIGID BODY OF FRANK MOVED EVER UP-WARD. MANY IN THE CROWD TURNED AWAY.

THOSE WHO CONTINUED TO WATCH SAW THE BODY FLOATING UP INTO THE SKY... UNTIL IT WAS NO MORE THAN A TINY SPECK...

...AND THEN... IT DISAPPEARED ALTOGETHER.

LEVITATION
by
Joseph Payne Brennan

Joseph Payne Brennan was born in 1918. He considers himself a poet, although he also writes fantasy and horror stories. For his poetry Brennan received the Leonora Speyer Memorial Award in 1961, for a book of poems called *New England Vignette*. He also won the World Fantasy Convention's award for life achievement in 1982. Some of his other stories are *Dark Harvest* and *Night Visions 2*. This story was adapted for the television series *Tales from the Dark Side*.

Now that you've read this story, ask yourself:

● Do you believe in levitation?

● Did you have any clue as to what was going to happen?

● Can you think of a possible ''next chapter'' for this plot?

THE TELL-TALE HEART

BY
EDGAR ALLAN POE

Story Adapted and
Illustrated by Rick Geary

19

20

I THINK IT WAS HIS EYE... YES, IT WAS THIS!

ONE OF THEM HAD A PALE BLUE FILM... IT MADE MY BLOOD RUN COLD!

GRADUALLY I MADE UP MY MIND TO TAKE THE OLD MAN'S LIFE... AND RID MYSELF OF THAT EYE FOREVER!

YOU STILL THINK ME MAD? BUT LOOK HOW SLOWLY AND CAUTIOUSLY I PROCEEDED.

I WAS NEVER KINDER TO THE OLD MAN THAN DURING THE WEEK BEFORE I KILLED HIM.

EVERY MIDNIGHT I WOULD OPEN HIS CHAMBER DOOR, OH SO GENTLY.

THEN I WOULD HOLD IN A LANTERN, ALL CLOSED SO THAT NO LIGHT SHONE OUT.

AND THEN I WOULD MOVE IN MY HEAD VERY SLOWLY...

SO SLOWLY IT TOOK ME AN HOUR TO PLACE MY WHOLE HEAD WITHIN THE OPENING.

WOULD A MADMAN DO THIS? CAUTIOUSLY, I UNDID THE DOOR OF THE LANTERN...

SO THAT A SINGLE RAY WOULD FALL UPON THAT HORRIBLE EYE.

FOR I DID NOT HATE THE OLD MAN... ONLY HIS EVIL EYE.

FOR SEVEN NIGHTS, I FOUND THE EYE CLOSED AND COULD NOT DO THE DEED.

ON THE EIGHTH NIGHT, I WAS MORE THAN USUALLY CAREFUL IN OPENING THE DOOR.

I FELT THE FULL EXTENT OF MY POWERS. I COULD HARDLY CONTAIN MY FEELINGS OF TRIUMPH, AND I CHUCKLED WITH GLEE IN SPITE OF MYSELF.

HE MUST HAVE HEARD ME, FOR SUDDENLY THE OLD MAN SPRANG UP IN BED. "WHO'S THERE?" HE CRIED.

FOR A WHOLE HOUR I STOOD STILL AND MADE NO SOUND.

IN THE MEANTIME, I DID NOT HEAR HIM LIE BACK DOWN.

HE WAS WAITING AND LISTENING IN THE BLACKNESS... AS WAS I! DEATH FILLED THE AIR.

AT LENGTH, I OPENED THE LANTERN THE TINIEST OF CRACKS.

A RAY SHOT OUT FULL UPON THE HORRID EYE!

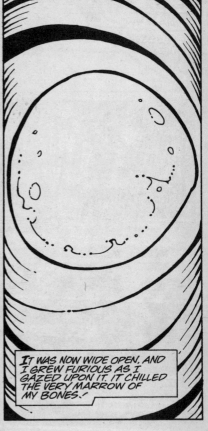

IT WAS NOW WIDE OPEN, AND I GREW FURIOUS AS I GAZED UPON IT. IT CHILLED THE VERY MARROW OF MY BONES!

NOW CAME TO MY EARS A LOW, DULL BEATING, AS OF A WATCH WRAPPED IN COTTON. IT WAS THE OLD MAN'S HEART.

EVEN THEN I REMAINED STILL... SO STILL I SCARCELY BREATHED.

BUT THE BEATING GREW LOUDER, EXCITING ME TO UNCONTROLLABLE TERROR.!

THEN A NEW FEAR SEIZED ME. WHAT IF A NEIGHBOR SHOULD HEAR THE DREADFUL SOUND? I DECIDED THE OLD MAN'S HOUR HAD COME.

SLOWLY, I SMOTHERED OUT HIS LIFE.

FOR MANY MINUTES THE HEART BEAT ON WITH A MUFFLED SOUND. AT LAST IT STOPPED. THE OLD MAN WAS DEAD.

HIS EYE WOULD BOTHER ME NO MORE.

IF YOU **STILL** THINK ME MAD, OBSERVE THE WISE PRECAUTIONS I NEXT TOOK.

FIRST I REMOVED THE CORPSE'S LIMBS.

I TOOK UP THREE PLANKS OF FLOORING AND DEPOSITED ALL THEREIN!

I THEN REPLACED THE FLOORING AND ARRANGED THE CHAMBER AS IF NOTHING HAD HAPPENED.

30

WHEN I HAD FINISHED THESE LABORS, IT WAS 4 A.M.

SOON, THERE CAME A KNOCKING AT THE STREET DOOR.

THERE I FOUND THREE MEN... OFFICERS OF THE POLICE! A CRY, THEY SAID, HAD BEEN HEARD BY NEIGHBORS.

I SMILED. WHAT HAD I TO FEAR?

I BADE THEM WELCOME. THE CRY HAD BEEN MY OWN, IN A DREAM, I SAID.

I TOLD THEM THE OLD MAN WAS AWAY IN THE COUNTRY AND SHOWED THEM HIS UNDISTURBED CHAMBER.

IN MY CONFIDENCE, I INVITED THEM TO SIT AND REST THEMSELVES.

I PLACED MY CHAIR OVER THE VERY SPOT WHERE I HAD CONCEALED THE VICTIM!

THE OFFICERS, APPARENTLY SATISFIED, CHATTED ABOUT FAMILIAR THINGS.

BUT SOON I WISHED THEM GONE...A MUFFLED SOUND CAME TO MY EARS.

IT WAS A LOW, DULL BEATING... GROWING STEADILY LOUDER!

I SPOKE FASTER, TURNING PALE, GASPING FOR BREATH.

YET, THE MEN STILL CONVERSED PLEASANTLY AS IF NOTHING WERE AMISS!

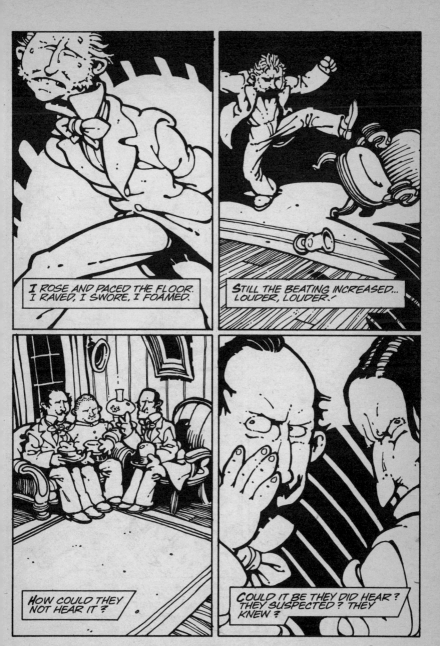

I ROSE AND PACED THE FLOOR. I RAVED, I SWORE, I FOAMED.

STILL THE BEATING INCREASED... LOUDER, LOUDER!

HOW COULD THEY NOT HEAR IT?

COULD IT BE THEY DID HEAR? THEY SUSPECTED? THEY KNEW?

THEY WERE MOCKING MY HORROR! I COULD BEAR THEIR SMILES NO LONGER!

LOUDER! LOUDER! IT WAS INTOLERABLE! I FELT I MUST SCREAM OR DIE!

"VILLAINS! I ADMIT THE DEED! TEAR UP THE PLANKS...

"HERE, HERE! IT IS THE BEATING OF HIS HIDEOUS HEART!"

THE TELL-TALE HEART
by
Edgar Allan Poe

Edgar Allan Poe, who lived in the 1800s, was one of America's greatest poets and writers. He was born very poor, and led a sad and troubled life. This may explain some of the gloomy and gruesome ideas in his work.

Poe was a master of terror. Among his short stories are "The Gold Bug" and "The Fall of the House of Usher." His most famous poem is "The Raven," and he loved to recite it at parties.

"The Tell-Tale Heart," a Poe classic, is about a murderer and his imagination.

Now that you've read this story, ask yourself:

- The story is told in the first person, as if by the murderer. Do you think this adds to the suspense or weakens it?

- Does Poe succeed in making you believe the man is truly mad?

- The heartbeat: Was it real? How do you explain what he heard?

JIMMY TAKES VANISHING LESSONS
BY
WALTER BROOKS

Story Adapted by Fred Schiller

Illustrated by Paul Mounts

39

40

41

HEY, WAIT A MINUTE! I SAW A GHOST... AND THAT'S SCARY AND ALL...

... BUT HE LAUGHED AT ME! JUST LIKE THAT BULLY AT SCHOOL WHO KNOCKS KIDS' BOOKS OUT OF THEIR HANDS-- AND THEN LAUGHS.

THAT GHOST IS NOTHING MORE THAN A BULLY-- AND I HATE BULLIES! I'M GOING BACK THERE AND TELL HIM SO!

BESIDES... I FORGOT TO TAKE AUNT MARY'S KEY!

44

I'LL TELL YOU WHAT. KEEP QUIET ABOUT THIS... AND I'LL TEACH YOU HOW TO VANISH!

WHY? WHAT GOOD WOULD THAT DO ME?

WHY, YOU COULD SNEAK INTO MOVIES WITHOUT PAYING!

I'M NOT A SNEAK.

OR I CAN SHOW YOU HOW TO BECOME MIST AND FLY THROUGH KEYHOLES!

WELL...

YOU MUST PROMISE NOT TO TELL ANYONE THAT YOU SCARED ME... PLEASE?

OKAY... I PROMISE.

I'LL BE BACK FOR THE LESSONS.

I'LL BE HERE! Heh-Heh-Heh!

46

TWO WEEKS LATER, IN AUNT MARY'S HOUSE...

COME ALONG, JIMMY... YOUR DINNER'S GETTING COLD.

JIMMY... WHAT IN THE WORLD DO YOU DO UP AT GRAND-FATHER'S HOUSE? YOU'RE THERE ALMOST EVERY DAY.

I'M TRYING TO GET RID OF THAT OLD GHOST. HE'S TAUGHT ME SOME NEAT STUFF, THOUGH.

NOW THAT'S ENOUGH OF... EEEEEK!!

IT'S OKAY, AUNT MARY-- I'M RIGHT HERE!

LISTEN... HE MAY BE A GHOST-- BUT HE'S REALLY NOT A BAD SORT. AND I THINK I KNOW HOW WE CAN GET RID OF HIM AND START RENTING THE HOUSE AGAIN.

47

AUNT MARY LISTENED TO JIMMY'S PLAN. THE NEXT DAY THEY TRIED IT.

WHO IN THE WORLD'S MAKING ALL THE RACKET, AND KICKING UP ALL THE DUST DOWN HERE?!

Oh, MY--A GHOST!

YOU BET YOUR FALSE TEETH I'M A GHOST!! NOW MOVE ALONG, BEFORE I REALLY--

BOO!

AWWK!! WHAT'S THAT?

Oh, MY... HEE HEE... A GHOST WHO'S AFRAID!

JIMMY! I MIGHT HAVE FIGURED THAT YOU'D BREAK YOUR WORD.

BUT I DIDN'T! YOU'RE THE ONE WHO SHOWED AUNT MARY THAT YOU'RE A SCARDEY CAT! NOT ME.

AND IF YOU DON'T WANT AUNT MARY TELLING EVERYONE SHE KNOWS--AND THEM TELLING EVERYONE THEY KNOW--YOU'D BETTER FIND ANOTHER HOUSE TO HAUNT.

AND SO THE GHOST DID JUST THAT.

AND AUNT MARY WAS ABLE TO RENT THE HOUSE TO A FINE, YOUNG FAMILY. BUT THAT'S NOT THE LAST JIMMY AND HIS AUNT SAW OF THE GHOST!

49

THAT'S IT, JIMMY... YOU'RE GETTING IT. CONCENTRATE!

HOW'S THIS?

YOU'RE GETTING IT, SON. THAT'S ALMOST AS GOOD AS A GHOST!

THAT'S ENOUGH OF THAT, YOU TWO. DINNER'S READY.

I GOT AN "A" ON MY CIVIL WAR TEST AT SCHOOL TODAY, AUNT MARY.

SMALL WONDER. YOU'VE GOT YOUR OWN PRIVATE TEACHER.

AND HE DID. FOR AFTER HE'D SPENT THE WINTER WITH THEM, JIMMY AND HIS AUNT INVITED HIM TO LIVE WITH THEM. AUNT MARY THOUGHT IT MIGHT BE FUN TO TAKE VANISHING LESSONS, TOO. AFTER ALL, YOU'RE NEVER TOO OLD TO LEARN.

JIMMY TAKES VANISHING LESSONS
by
Walter R. Brooks

Walter R. Brooks is a British writer who spe-
cializes in fantasy and humor. His stories have
fun with the usual fantasy plot lines.

One of his tales, "Like a Diamond in the Sky,"
tells of a man named Simpson who battles an el-
derly wizard. The wizard casts a spell on Simpson,
who loses weight and finally drifts off into thin
air. Another story, "Whitcomb's Genie," is about
a New England farmer who finds a lamp complete
with a magic genie.

In "Jimmy Takes Vanishing Lessons," Brooks
created a ghost of still another kind.

Now that you've read this story, ask yourself:

- If you were Jimmy, would you have
  checked out the haunted house?

- What makes this ghost story funny rather
  than scary?

- What is your special reason for reading
  fantasy and ghost stories?

THE OTHER WING
BY
ALGERNON BLACKWOOD

Story Adapted and Illustrated
by Frederic Lere

1881. EAST OF BIRMINGHAM, ENGLAND. YOUNG TIM SHREWSBURY, RECENTLY MARRIED, HAS INHERITED THE FAMILY MANSION AFTER HIS PARENTS' DEATH.

I HAVEN'T BEEN BACK HOME IN TWENTY YEARS-- BUT NOTHING'S CHANGED!

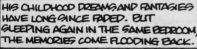

HIS CHILDHOOD DREAMS AND FANTASIES HAVE LONG SINCE FADED. BUT SLEEPING AGAIN IN THE SAME BEDROOM, THE MEMORIES COME FLOODING BACK.

THE SAME CURTAIN. I REMEMBER HOW I USED TO COUNT THE ANIMALS ON IT-- BUT I NEVER GOT THE SAME COUNT TWICE.

?!

TIM, I FEEL A PRESENCE IN THIS HOUSE. LAST NIGHT, BEFORE YOU SAVED US FROM THE FIRE, I SAW A GHOST... OR DREAMED OF ONE.

YES... I SAW HIM AS WELL.

IT WAS MY GRANDFATHER -- AND IT WAS HE WHO SAVED BOTH OF US.

YOUR GRANDFATHER'S GHOST? HOW EXCITING!

THIS PORTRAIT -- WHY, THAT'S THE GHOST! EVEN THE SAME CANE!

YES... THE ONE MISSING FROM THE STICK RACK.

GRANDFATHER'S CANE... YES -- IT ALL COMES BACK TO ME NOW.

55

56

A GHOST! IT MUST HAVE COME THROUGH THE NIGHTMARE PASSAGE. BUT IT'S SO BEAUTIFUL, IT CAN'T BE A NIGHTMARE!

"AT SEVEN, I ALREADY HAD STRONG IDEAS ABOUT DREAMS AND NIGHTMARES... AND THE CREATURES WHO ATTENDED THEM."

SHE IS MY NIGHTTIME GUARDIAN... I'LL DREAM OF HER.

"I WAS CERTAIN THAT, EACH NIGHT AS I SLEPT, THERE WAS A PRESENCE IN MY BEDROOM.

"THEY WERE FRIENDLY, PROTECTIVE. I DECIDED TO TELL THE GROWN-UPS.

"FIRST, I TOLD MY NANNY."

YOU SEE, THE BIG ONE COMES ALONG FIRST, AND WHEN I'M ASLEEP, SHE BRINGS THE LITTLE ONES.

SO THE QUICKER YOU SLEEP, THE BETTER!

57

"SHE DIDN'T BELIEVE ME. I SPOKE WITH MY FATHER NEXT."

OF COURSE. IT IS "SLEEP," COMING TO CARRY YOU AWAY TO THE LAND OF DREAMS. NOW, LEAVE ME TO MY WORK. RUN AND ASK YOUR MOTHER ABOUT IT.

YOU SEE-- SHE IS SOMEONE REAL.

AND SHE TAKES CARE OF YOU. THAT'S LOVELY, TIM.

OH, YES, I KNOW, BUT...

YOUR FATHER IS RIGHT. SHE IS "SLEEP." AND SHE HAS WINGS-- I'VE ALWAYS HEARD THAT.

THEN, THE LITTLE ONES. WHAT ARE THEY?

PERHAPS THEY ARE DREAMS.

DREAMS? OF COURSE! AND I KNOW WHERE THEY MUST STAY DURING THE DAY-- IN THE OTHER WING!

"FOR MANY YEARS, THE OTHER WING HAD BEEN CLOSED UP. OUR MANSION WAS MUCH TOO HUGE FOR OUR SMALL, MODERN FAMILY."

THE OTHER WING! I KNOW THEY ARE IN THERE -- SLEEP, THE RULER, AND HER LITTLE DREAMS -- WAITING FOR DARKNESS!

COME BACK, TIM! WE'RE GOING TO PLAY DOWN BY THE STREAM!

"I HAD NO USE FOR GAMES WITH OTHER CHILDREN. I HAD ONLY ONE INTEREST -- THE OTHER WING AND ITS INHABITANTS.

"I WATCHED FOR HOURS, HOPING TO SEE SLEEP AS SHE LEFT TO VISIT THE OTHER CHILDREN IN THE WORLD. FOR, SURELY, SLEEP MUST VISIT EVERYONE."

TIM, IT'S GETTING DARK. COME INSIDE!

59

"I PEERED THROUGH THE SHUTTERS AND DIMLY SAW THE LONG HALLWAY THAT LED TO THE OTHER WING. IN MY MIND, IT WAS THE NIGHTMARE PASSAGE.

"I FELT I KNEW IT INTIMATELY. IT WAS INSIDE MYSELF, AS WELL AS BEHIND CLOSED DOORS."

YOU'RE IN THERE! I CAN HEAR YOU WHISPERING!

"I MADE UP MY MIND. I HAD TO GO IN THERE AND MEET SLEEP IN HER OWN PLACE."

WHERE HAVE YOU BEEN? IT'S ALMOST BEDTIME!

"I KNEW THERE WOULD BE PROBLEMS WITH THE GROWN-UPS, SO I DECIDED NOT TO TELL THEM."

"AND SO, THE NEXT MORNING...

"I DECIDED ON A DAYLIGHT VISIT -- TO MEET SLEEP WHILE SHE PREPARED FOR HER NIGHTLY JOURNEY.

TOO HIGH!

"I COULD NOT GET IN FROM THE OUTSIDE. I WOULD HAVE TO GO THROUGH THE NIGHTMARE PASSAGE TO THE OTHER WING.

"EARLY ONE EVENING, I NOTICED AN OPEN DOOR... IT HAD ALWAYS BEEN CLOSED BEFORE.

"I LONGED TO SEE HER -- TO TELL HER THAT I BELIEVED IN HER ... THAT I LOVED HER."

TIM! COME KISS US GOOD-BYE!

!!

61

WE'LL BE BACK LATE TONIGHT.

NANNY WILL TAKE CARE OF YOU. BE A GOOD BOY!

"THIS WAS MY CHANCE. I HAD TWO HOURS BEFORE BEDTIME!

"I STARTED MY JOURNEY BY EXPLORING ANOTHER ROOM THAT HAD LONG BEEN FORBIDDEN TO ME -- MY FATHER'S STUDY."

WHAT A WONDERFUL ROOM!

A PICTURE OF GRANDFATHER! IF HE WERE STILL ALIVE, HE'D BE OVER A HUNDRED BY NOW. I'M SORRY I NEVER GOT TO MEET HIM.

HERE, IN THE RACK -- IT'S THE SAME CANE AS IN THE PORTRAIT!

62

63

65

"AS I WATCHED, THE REED FADED... THE CANE RETURNED."

"I WAS FROZEN WITH FEAR. THEN, *SHE* WAS THERE."

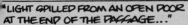

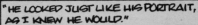

67

68

69

RAGAMUFFIN! YOU'VE BEEN ASLEEP IN MY STUDY! WELL... I GUESS YOU'RE OLD ENOUGH TO BE ALLOWED IN HERE NOW.

EH... WHAT'S THIS? FATHER'S STICK--- IT'S MISSING!

WHERE IS IT? DID YOU TAKE IT? ANSWER ME, TIM!

I...I... DON'T KNOW...

IT COULDN'T JUST VANISH! TIM--TELL ME THE TRUTH.

I SWEAR, FATHER--I DON'T KNOW WHERE THE STICK IS!

"WHICH WAS, DEAR MOIRA, OF COURSE THE TRUTH. NO ONE EVER SAW IT AGAIN...UNTIL LAST NIGHT, WHEN GRANDFATHER RETURNED TO REPAY THE FAVOR."

70

THE OTHER WING
by
Algernon Blackwood

Algernon Blackwood was England's leading writer of supernatural stories in the early 1900s. He was a great camper and mountain climber who loved nature and the outdoors. Later in his life he became well known on British TV.

Blackwood wrote hundreds of ghost stories. They were published in collections such as *The Empty House, The Listener, The Lost Valley, The Minute Stories,* and *Pam's Garden.*

"The Other Wing" is a ghost story set in an old English manor house. The place has a secret wing—and now you know its secret.

Now that you've read this story, ask yourself:

- What object was the link between Tim and his ghostly grandfather?

- If you were Tim, would you have gone into the mysterious "other wing"?

- What's another way that the story could have ended?

*T*HE *G*REATEST *G*IFT

BY
PHILIP VAN DOREN STERN

Story Adapted by Howard Zimmerman

Illustrated by Alex Nino

THE LITTLE TOWN ON THE HILL WAS BRIGHT WITH COLORED CHRISTMAS LIGHTS AND ALIVE WITH THE SOUND OF CAROLING CHILDREN.

BUT GEORGE PRATT DID NOT SEE OR HEAR THEM, AS HE WATCHED BITS OF ICE FLOATING DOWNSTREAM TO BE SWALLOWED BY THE SHADOWS.

THE WATER LOOKED DEADLY COLD. GEORGE WONDERED HOW LONG A MAN COULD STAY ALIVE IN ITS SWIRLING CURRENTS.

73

THE GLASSY BLACKNESS HAD A STRANGE, HYP-NOTIC EFFECT ON HIM. HE LEANED STILL FARTHER OVER THE RAILING.

I WOULDN'T DO THAT IF I WERE YOU!

GEORGE TURNED TOWARD THE LITTLE MAN. HE WAS CARRYING A SMALL BLACK SATCHEL, LIKE A SALESMAN'S SAMPLE KIT.

HOW DO YOU KNOW WHAT I WAS THINKING OF DOING?

OH, IT'S OUR BUSINESS TO KNOW OF THESE THINGS. IT'S CHRISTMAS EVE. CON-SIDER HOW MARY WOULD FEEL... AND YOUR MOTHER, TOO.

GEORGE STARTED TO PROTEST, BUT WAS HALTED BY THE KNOWING LOOK IN THE STRANGER'S BRIGHT BLUE EYES.

HRRMMPH! SINCE YOU KNOW SO MUCH ABOUT ME, GIVE ME ONE GOOD REASON WHY I SHOULDN'T JUMP?

YOU'VE GOT YOUR JOB AT THE BANK, AND MARY AND THE KIDS. YOU'RE HEALTHY, YOUNG, AND...

AND SICK OF EVERYTHING. I'M STUCK IN THIS MUDHOLE, DOING THE SAME DULL WORK DAY AFTER DAY. I'VE NEVER DONE ANY-THING USEFUL OR INTERESTING. SOME-TIMES I WISH I'D NEVER BEEN BORN.

GREAT! THAT SOLVES EVERYTHING. I WAS AFRAID YOU WERE GOING TO BE TROUBLE. BUT NOW YOU'VE GIVEN ME THE SOLUTION. YOU WISH YOU'D NEVER BEEN BORN... OKAY!! YOU HAVEN'T.

WHAT DO YOU MEAN?

JUST THAT. YOU HAVEN'T BEEN BORN. NO ONE KNOWS YOU. YOU HAVE NO RESPONSIBILI-TIES--NO JOB--NO WIFE--NO CHILDREN. WHY, YOU DON'T EVEN HAVE A MOTHER.

YOUR WISH HAS BEEN GRANTED-- OFFICIALLY.

GEORGE LAUGHED AND TURNED AWAY. THE STRANGER RAN AFTER HIM AND CAUGHT HIM BY THE ARM.

YOU'D BETTER TAKE THIS WITH YOU. IT'LL OPEN A LOT OF DOORS THAT MIGHT OTHERWISE BE SLAMMED IN YOUR FACE.

WHAT ARE YOU TALKING ABOUT? I KNOW EVERYBODY IN THIS TOWN.

YES, I KNOW. THAT'S WHY YOU'LL BE SURPRISED HOW USEFUL THESE FREE BRUSHES CAN BE.

AND WHEN YOU GIVE THEM AWAY, THIS IS WHAT I WANT YOU TO SAY...

GEORGE LISTENED ABSENTLY TO THE INSTRUC-TIONS WHILE HE FUMBLED WITH ONE OF THE BRUSHES. BUT WHEN HE LOOKED UP, GEORGE SHIVERED, TURNED UP HIS COAT COLLAR, AND HURRIED BACK TOWARD TOWN, STILL HOLDING THE LITTLE MAN'S BLACK BAG.

WHEN HE REACHED THE BANK WHERE HE WORKED, HE SAW THAT THE BUILD-ING WAS DARK. ODD! HE HAD TURNED THE LIGHTS ON BEFORE HE LEFT.

HE RAN AROUND TO THE FRONT. THERE WAS A STRANGE SIGN HANGING IN THE DOORWAY. THE BUILDING LOOKED RUN-DOWN AND DIRTY... AND IT WAS NO LONGER THE BANK HE HAD WORKED IN.

FOR RENT OR SALE

APPLY JAMES SILVA REAL ESTATE

A LIGHT WAS STILL BURNING ACROSS THE STREET IN JIM SILVA'S OFFICE. GEORGE DASHED OVER AND TORE THE DOOR OPEN. JIM GREETED HIM POLITELY, AS THOUGH HE HAD NEVER SEEN GEORGE BEFORE.

WHY IS THE BANK FOR RENT?

IT'S BEEN FOR RENT EVER SINCE IT WENT BUST. A GOOD NINE OR TEN YEARS AGO. ARE YOU INTERESTED IN RENTING IT?

I WAS HERE SOME TIME AGO, AND THE BANK WAS ALL RIGHT THEN. I EVEN KNEW SOME OF THE PEOPLE WHO WORKED THERE.

DIDN'T KNOW A FELLER NAMED MARTY JENKINS, DID YOU?

GEORGE WAS ABOUT TO SAY THAT MARTY HAD NEVER WORKED AT THE BANK. THEY BOTH HAD APPLIED FOR THE JOB SOON AFTER HIGH SCHOOL, AND GEORGE HAD GOTTEN IT.

76

"NO, I DIDN'T KNOW HIM. HEARD OF HIM VAGUELY. WHY?"

"THOUGHT MAYBE YOU HEARD HOW HE SKIPPED OUT WITH FIFTY THOUSAND DOLLARS. PRETTY NEAR RUINED EVERYONE AROUND HERE. THAT'S WHY THE BANK WENT BROKE."

"DIDN'T HE HAVE A BROTHER NAMED ARTHUR?"

"YEAH, BUT ART DIDN'T KNOW ANYTHING ABOUT IT. HAD A BAD EFFECT ON HIM, THOUGH. TOOK TO DRINKING. REAL HARD ON HIS WIFE. NICE GIRL, TOO."

GEORGE BOLTED OUT OF THE OFFICE WITHOUT LISTENING TO THE REST. HE HAD A SINKING FEELING IN HIS STOMACH. BOTH HE AND ART HAD COURTED MARY.

FOR A MOMENT, HE THOUGHT OF GOING STRAIGHT TO MARY, BUT HE COULDN'T FACE HER-- NOT YET, ANYWAY. HE DECIDED TO VISIT HIS PARENTS FIRST.

"BROWNIE, STOP THAT, YOU OLD FOOL. DON'T YOU KNOW ME?"

THE PORCH LIGHT SNAPPED ON, AND GEORGE'S FATHER STEPPED OUT. GEORGE COULD SEE BY THE WAY HIS FATHER LOOKED AT HIM THAT HE DIDN'T KNOW WHO HE WAS.

"HELLO, IS THE LADY OF THE HOUSE IN?"

"GO ON IN. JUST LET ME CHAIN THE DOG UP. SHE CAN BE REAL MEAN WITH STRANGERS."

77

GOOD EVENING, MA'AM, I'M FROM THE WORLD CLEANING COMPANY. WE'RE GIVING OUT FREE SAMPLE BRUSHES, AND I THOUGHT YOU MIGHT LIKE TO HAVE ONE.

HOW NICE, BUT NOW I SUPPOSE YOU'LL WANT TO SELL ME SOMETHING.

NO, MA'AM, I'M NOT TRYING TO SELL ANYTHING. THIS IS A CHRISTMAS PRESENT FROM THE COMPANY.

WELL, THANK YOU, AND MERRY CHRISTMAS TO YOU. CAN I GET YOU A CUP OF TEA OR SOMETHING? YOU DO LOOK TIRED.

GEORGE LOOKED AROUND THE LITTLE PARLOR. IT LOOKED DIFFERENT SOMEHOW, BUT HE COULDN'T FIGURE OUT WHY.

I USED TO KNOW THIS TOWN PRETTY WELL. I REMEMBER A GIRL NAMED MARY THATCHER. DO YOU KNOW HER?

OF COURSE, LOVELY GIRL. MARRIED ART JENKINS, TWO BEAUTIFUL CHILDREN.

GEORGE GROANED.

SUDDENLY GEORGE NOTICED THE PHOTOGRAPH THAT HUNG OVER THE MANTEL. IT HAD BEEN OF HIM AND HIS KID BROTHER. NOW, ONLY HARRY WAS IN THE PHOTO. THAT'S WHY THE ROOM SEEMED DIFFERENT.

THAT YOUR SON? I THINK I KNOW HIM. NAME'S HARRY, RIGHT?

HIS MOTHER'S FACE CLOUDED. SHE NODDED BUT SAID NOTHING.

YOU COULDN'T HAVE MET HIM. HE'S BEEN DEAD A LONG WHILE. HE WAS DROWNED THE DAY THAT PICTURE WAS TAKEN.

GEORGE'S MIND FLEW BACK TO WHEN THAT PHOTO HAD BEEN TAKEN. ON THEIR WAY HOME, THEY HAD STOPPED FOR A SWIM. HARRY CAUGHT A CRAMP, AND GEORGE PULLED HIM FROM THE WATER. NOTHING TO IT. ONLY THIS TIME, GEORGE HADN'T BEEN THERE TO PULL HARRY OUT.

I'M SORRY. I GUESS I'D BETTER GO. I HOPE YOU LIKE THE BRUSH. I WISH YOU BOTH A MERRY CHRISTMAS.

AS HE SAID IT, BOTH PARENTS STARTED TO WEEP, AND GEORGE FLEW FROM THE HOUSE IN GRIEF.

HE WANTED DESPERATELY TO SEE MARY. HE WASN'T SURE HE COULD STAND NOT BEING RECOGNIZED BY HER, BUT HE HAD TO TAKE THE CHANCE.

HE STUMBLED BLINDLY UP THE PATH TO HIS OWN HOUSE. THE BEAUTIFUL LAWN WAS NOW A MESS, AND HIS PRIZE FLOWER BUSHES WERE BADLY KEPT. EASY TO SEE THAT ART JENKINS WAS LIVING THERE NOW.

MER-- MERRY CHRISTMAS, MA'AM. I HAVE A FREE GIFT FROM THE WORLD CLEANING COMPANY.

AT THE SIGHT OF HER, GEORGE'S VOICE ALMOST FAILED.

BUT HE GRINNED AS HE ENTERED THE PARLOR. THAT HIGH-PRICED BLUE SOFA THAT THEY OFTEN QUARRELED OVER WAS STILL THERE. MARY MUST HAVE HAD THE SAME FIGHT WITH ART AND WON IT WITH HIM, TOO.

GEORGE OPENED HIS SATCHEL. HE FOUND A BRUSH WITH A BRIGHT BLUE HANDLE AND MULTI-COLORED BRISTLES, AND HANDED IT TO MARY.

MY, THAT'S A PRETTY BRUSH. YOU'RE GIVING IT AWAY FREE?

SPECIAL INTRODUCTORY OFFER, IT'S A WAY FOR THE COMPANY TO MAKE NEW FRIENDS.

SHE STROKED THE SOFA GENTLY WITH THE BRUSH, SMOOTH-ING OUT THE VEL-VETY NAP.

IT'S A NICE BRUSH. THANK YOU. I...

MOMMY, MOMMY, HE'S AFTER ME! HE'S AFTER ME!

SHE WON'T DIE! I SHOT HER A HUNERT TIMES, BUT SHE WON'T DIE!

HUMPH! LOOKS JUST LIKE ART JENKINS. ACTS LIKE HIM, TOO.

YOU'RE DEAD. WHY DON'T YOU FALL DOWN AND DIE?

SUDDENLY THE DOOR BANGED OPEN, AND THE LITTLE BOY BECAME QUIET. MARY GLANCED NERVOUSLY AT THE SWAYING FIGURE.

WHO'S THIS?

HE'S JUST A SALESMAN. HE GAVE ME A FREE BRUSH.

WELLL, TELL HIM TO GET OUTTA MY HOUSE. WE DON'T NEED NO BRUSHES, OR NO SALESMEN, NEITHER.

GEORGE LOOKED AT MARY. HER EYES BEGGED HIM TO GO.

PLEASE. YOU'LL HAVE TO LEAVE NOW.

GEORGE WENT TO THE DOOR, PURSUED BY ART'S SON.

BANG! YOU'RE DEAD-- DEAD--DEAD!

THE BOY WAS RIGHT, GEORGE THOUGHT. HE WAS DEAD. HE HAD TO FIND THAT LITTLE MAN AND GET HIM TO CANCEL THE TER- RIBLE DEAL HE'D MADE.

HE HURRIED FROM THE TOWN AND BROKE INTO A RUN. THE LITTLE MAN WAS SITTING ON THE BRIDGE, LOOKING AS IF HE'D NEVER LEFT.

I'VE HAD ENOUGH! GET ME OUT OF THIS MESS -- YOU GOT ME INTO IT.

I GOT YOU INTO! HA-HA! I ONLY GAVE YOU YOUR WISH, SON. YOU'RE NOW THE FREEST MAN ON EARTH. YOU CAN GO ANY-WHERE -- DO ANYTHING. WHAT MORE CAN YOU POSSIBLY WANT?

YOU DON'T UNDER-STAND. IT'S NOT FOR ME, IT'S FOR THE OTHERS. THIS TOWN'S A MESS. THEY NEED ME. I'VE GOT TO GET BACK.

YOU HAD THE GREATEST GIFT OF ALL -- THE GIFT OF LIFE. YET YOU DENIED THAT GIFT.

MARY NEEDS ME.

WELL, IT IS CHRISTMAS EVE. I SUPPOSE WE CAN BEND THE RULES A LITTLE.

CLOSE YOUR EYES AND LIS-TEN TO CHILDREN'S CAROLING CAR-RIED ON THE WIND.

KEEP LISTENING... AND REMEMBERING... AND NEVER LET IT GO AGAIN.

AND WHEN HE OPENED HIS EYES, THE LITTLE MAN WAS GONE.

GEORGE WAS SO FRANTIC WITH JOY AS HE RUSHED BACK TO TOWN THAT HE FAILED TO SEE JIM WALKING HIS WAY.

OOOF! HEY, WATCH WHERE YOU'RE GOING, YOU CLUMSY...

OH, HI, GEORGE. I ALMOST DIDN'T RECOGNIZE YOU.

BY THE WAY, YOU'VE WON THE PRIZE FROM THE CHAMBER OF COMMERCE--FOR THE CHRISTMAS SCENE YOU DID IN THE BANK WINDOW.

GEORGE THANKED HIM, WISHED HIM A MERRY CHRISTMAS, AND HURRIED OFF.

HE STOPPED BRIEFLY AT HIS PARENTS' HOUSE, WHERE HE WRESTLED WITH BROWNIE UNTIL THE FRIENDLY OLD BULLDOG WAGGLED ALL OVER WITH DELIGHT.

HE GRASPED HIS STARTLED BROTHER'S HAND AND WRUNG IT FRANTICALLY, WISHING HIM A HEARTY MERRY CHRISTMAS.

HE KISSED HIS MOTHER AND JOKED WITH HIS FATHER. HE WAS OUT OF THE HOUSE A FEW SECONDS LATER, STUMBLING AND SLIPPING AS HE RAN UP THE HILL.

83

WHEN HE FINALLY REACHED HIS HOME, GEORGE FLUNG THE DOOR OPEN AND STARTED SINGING CHRISTMAS CAROLS AT THE TOP OF HIS LUNGS.

SHHHH! YOU'LL WAKE THE CHILDREN. I'VE JUST PUT THEM TO BED.

MARY CHRISTMAS! MARY CHRISTMAS! HO! HO! HO!

IN A FLASH HE PUT HER DOWN AND WAS UP THE STAIRS TO THE KIDS' ROOM. MARY RAN AFTER HIM, PROTESTING ALL THE WAY.

BY THE TIME SHE CAUGHT UP WITH HIM, HE WAS MADLY EMBRACING HIS SON AND HIS DAUGHTER AND WAKING THEM THOROUGHLY.

IT WAS NOT UNTIL MARY GOT HIM DOWN-STAIRS THAT HE CAUGHT HIS BREATH AND HE BEGAN TO EXPLAIN.

OH, MARY, I THOUGHT I'D LOST YOU. WHAT A HORRIBLE NIGHT-MARE I HAD.

DARLING, I DON'T UNDER-STAND. WHAT IS IT?

HE PULLED HER DOWN ON THE SOFA AND KISSED HER AGAIN. JUST AS HE WAS ABOUT TO TELL HER ABOUT HIS TERRIBLE DREAM, HIS FINGERS CAME IN CONTACT WITH SOMETHING LYING ON THE SEAT TO THE SOFA. HIS HEART JUMPED...

...AND SUDDENLY, HE DIDN'T KNOW WHERE TO BEGIN.

THE GREATEST GIFT
by
Philip van Doren Stern

Philip van Doren Stern comes from a literary family. Most of his writing deals with the field of American history, but he also likes to write supernatural tales, for a "change of pace." Among his books are *The Man Who Killed Lincoln, An End to Valor,* about the last days of the Civil War, and *The Other Side of the Clock,* a collection of his unusual ghost stories.

"The Greatest Gift" tells of a man named George Pratt who's reached the end of his rope and is thinking of committing suicide. This tale was the basis for a famous movie with James Stewart entitled *It's a Wonderful Life.*

Now that you've read this story, ask yourself:

- Have you ever felt really "down," the way George did? What did you do about it?

- What if you hadn't been born? Can you think of one thing that would have been very different in your family?

- Can you think of one person who has or had a big influence in your life?

THE HOUSE OF THE NIGHTMARE

BY
EDWARD L. WHITE

Story Adapted by Fred Schiller

Illustrated by Robin Ator
and Gary Kato

IT WAS THE FIRST VACATION I'D HAD IN YEARS AND I WAS ENJOYING MY TOUR OF SOUTHERN ROADS.

I SHOULDN'T HAVE BEEN TRAVELING ALONE--BUT I HAD NO IDEA OF WHAT WAS IN STORE FOR ME.

I DIDN'T HAVE A CARE IN THE WORLD--JUST MILES OF OPEN ROAD BEFORE ME.

I SPOTTED A FARMHOUSE AHEAD, ON THE LEFT SIDE OF THE ROAD...

WHICH, WHEN NEXT I SAW IT, HAD MOVED TO THE RIGHT SIDE OF THE ROAD.

WAS IT ONLY A TRICK OF THE SUN? I DECIDED TO INVESTIGATE.

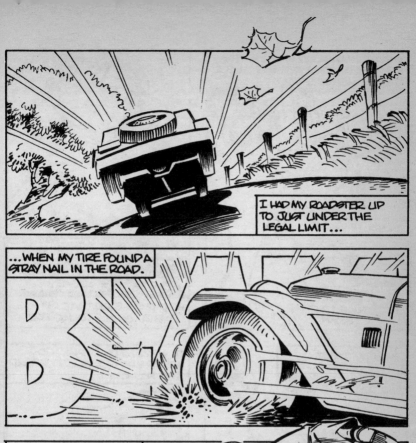

I HAD MY ROADSTER UP TO JUST UNDER THE LEGAL LIMIT...

...WHEN MY TIRE FOUND A STRAY NAIL IN THE ROAD.

MY FLIGHT WAS SHORT-- A STURDY OAK TREE STOPPED MY FALL.

KRUNCH!

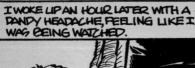
I WOKE UP AN HOUR LATER WITH A DANDY HEADACHE, FEELING LIKE I WAS BEING WATCHED.

HAVE A NICE TRIP? HAW!

THE COMIC WAS A LOCAL BOY-- WHO NEVER DID TELL ME HIS NAME.

HE DID TELL ME THAT I'D CRASHED ON HIS FOLKS' FARM.

I WANTED TO GET MY CAR TO A GARAGE-- BUT THE CLOSEST ONE WAS OVER TEN MILES AWAY.

IT WAS GETTING DARK, SO I ASKED HIM IF I COULD SPEND THE NIGHT.

SURE... I GUESS.

90

91

THE INSIDE WAS NO BETTER. EVERYTHING WAS THICK WITH DUST.

BUT AT LEAST THE SPARE BEDROOM HAD A SOFT BED.

AND THE KITCHEN HAD A BIG FIREPLACE, IN WHICH I BUILT A ROARING FIRE.

THE SHELVES WERE EMPTY, SO USING THE FOOD I'D BROUGHT, I MADE US DINNER.

SOUP'S ON SPORT! DIG IN!

NAW...I'M NOT HUNGRY. FIRE'S GOOD...HOT.

SUDDENLY, I WASN'T VERY HUNGRY MYSELF.

AS HE HUGGED THE FLAMES, I ASKED IF HE HAD MANY FRIENDS.

NAW...NO ONE COMES AROUND HERE MUCH ANYMORE. THEY'RE ALL AFRAID OF THE GHOSTS.

THE GHOSTS DON'T BOTHER ME MUCH ANYMORE -- MOSTLY, IT'S THE SPOOKY DREAMS THAT GET ME.

93

94

THE ONLY THING I FELT WAS SLEEPY... SO I DOZED OFF.

I WOKE WHEN SOMETHING SOFT BRUSHED ACROSS MY FACE.

HEY! WAS THAT YOU, KID?!

NAW... BEEN SITTING RIGHT HERE. HAD TO HAVE BEEN ONE OF THE GHOSTS-- THE LADY WITH THE VEIL.

I THINK IT'S MY MOM.

IT TOOK A WHILE AFTER THAT, BUT I GOT SLEEPY AGAIN.

AND THE BED WAS SOFT.

THE DREAM CAME RIGHT AWAY... AND IT WAS BAD.

96

97

THE ROOM SHOOK AS IT NEARED ME.

FEAR SWALLOWED ME WHOLE, AND I WAS FROZEN IN BED.

THE CREATURE'S BREATH STANK OF DEATH, AND I WAS ABOUT TO LOSE MY MIND COMPLETELY...

YaaaaAa *

BUT THEN, I SCREAMED MYSELF AWAKE AGAIN.

BEING ONE TO LEARN FROM MY MISTAKES, I QUICKLY CHECKED THE ROOM.

AFTER WHICH I PACKED MY BAGS...

... AND WAS OUT OF THE HOUSE IN MERE MINUTES. MY YOUNG HOST WAS NOWHERE TO BE FOUND.

WITH THE RISING SUN AS A COMPASS, I HEADED FOR THE NEAREST TOWN.

FIVE HOURS LATER, I REACHED IT.

GOOD DAY, SIR. COULD YOU SPARE SOME WATER?

WELL, SURE, YOUNG FELLER! DID YOUR CAR BREAK DOWN ON YOU?

SOMETHING LIKE THAT... TEN MILES BACK, AT THE NEXT FARM. A YOUNG BOY LET ME SPEND THE NIGHT.

WHAT? YOU MUST BE MIXED UP-- OR THE HEAT'S GOT YOU. HAS TO BE!

THIS WAS A BIG WHITE HOUSE, WITH A SILO IN BACK. COMING UP, I COULDN'T TELL WHICH SIDE OF THE ROAD IT WAS ON.

WELL, THAT SOUNDS RIGHT, BUT NO ONE'S LIVED UP THERE FOR YEARS! THE WHOLE FAMILY'S DEAD. THE PLACE IS SPOOKED!

THE BOY SAID THAT HIS MOTHER DIED THREE YEARS AGO...

THAT SHE DID, MISTER-- BUT THEN THE BOY HIMSELF DIED A YEAR LATER!

THE HOUSE OF THE NIGHTMARE
by
Edward L. White

Edward L. White was a teacher as well as a writer. He is best known for his historical novels, which are heavy on facts. But White also wrote light fantasies. Among these are *Floki's Blade* and *The Picture Puzzle*, a tale of magic in China. He also wrote *Sorcery Island*, which is about island people held in slavery by a warlock who dresses as a gigantic bird!

''The House of the Nightmare'' is a combination ghost story and fantasy tale, set in the 1920s. The plot doesn't seem unusual . . . until you reach the ending.

Now that you've read this story, ask yourself:

- Do you believe in ghosts? Have you ever seen any?

- What was the meaning of the large, white stone that moved from side to side across the road?

- What do you think about staying overnight in this house? Would you have done it?

THE COUNTRY
OF THE BLIND
BY
H. G. WELLS

Story Adapted and Illustrated
by Frederic Lere

IT CAN'T BE... BUT IT IS! A HIDDEN VILLAGE. I'M SAVED.

NIGHT FELL WITH SUDDEN SWIFTNESS. NUNEZ COULD NOT RISK GOING ANY FURTHER.

STRANGE, THAT THERE ARE NO LIGHTS FROM THE VILLAGE. CAN'T BE TOO FAR AWAY, THOUGH. I'LL SLEEP HERE.

BUT BEFORE LONG...

NOISES, FROM THE DARK! SOUNDS LIKE PEOPLE. BUT WHAT CAN THEY BE UP TO IN THE MIDDLE OF THE NIGHT?

NUNEZ QUIETLY FOLLOWED THE SOUNDS. BY MORNING, HE HAD ARRIVED AT THE VILLAGE. IT WAS COMPLETELY CUT OFF FROM THE REST OF THE WORLD. EVEN HIS PATH DOWN THE MOUNTAIN HAD BEEN ERASED BY THE BLOWING SNOWS.

HEL-LO!

THEY CAN HEAR ME, BUT THEY CAN'T SEE ME! THIS MUST BE THE LEGENDARY "COUNTRY OF THE BLIND."

AND IN THE LAND OF THE BLIND, EVEN A ONE-EYED MAN CAN BE KING!

IS IT MAN OR SPIRIT, WHO COMES DOWN FROM THE ROCKS?

108

109

PLEASE... TURN ON A LIGHT. I CAN'T SEE ANYTHING IN THIS GLOOM.

HIS NAME IS BOGOTÁ. HE NEEDS OUR HELP. HE HAS TROUBLE WALKING, AND SPEAKS NONSENSE.

CAN YOU UNDERSTAND WHAT WE ARE SAYING, BOGOTÁ?

MY NAME IS NUÑEZ. BOGOTÁ IS A CITY, FROM THE WORLD BEYOND YOUR VILLAGE... WHERE MEN HAVE EYES, AND CAN SEE.

EYES,... SEE? BOGOTÁ, YOU MUST LEARN THE TRUTH OF THE WORLD. IT IS AN EMPTY SPACE, BETWEEN THE ROCKS. IN IT LIVE THE THINGS THAT GROW BUT CANNOT SPEAK. AND THE LLAMAS, WHO WORK FOR MEN. AND LASTLY THERE ARE THE ANGELS. THEY SING WHEN IT IS WARM, BUT NO ONE CAN TOUCH THEM.

SINGING ANGELS? HE MUST MEAN BIRDS.

TIME IS DIVIDED INTO THE WARM AND THE COLD. WE SLEEP BY THE WARM, AND WORK BY COLD. NOW YOU MUST REST, AND THEN TRY TO LEARN. BUT FIRST, YOU MUST HAVE SOME FOOD.

THEY WILL HAVE TO LEARN! I, WHO HAVE THE POWER OF SIGHT, SHALL BE THEIR KING! BUT HOW WILL I CONVINCE THEM...?

AT SUNSET, NUNEZ HAD A VISITOR.

HELLO, BOGOTÁ! I AM YACOB. THE ELDERS PUT ME IN CHARGE OF YOU. COME!

HERE'S MY CHANCE! WITHOUT EYES, HE WILL NEVER FIND ME...

BOGOTÁ! DON'T STEP ON THE GRASS. IT IS FORBIDDEN.

BUT I BARELY MADE ANY NOISE AT ALL!

LISTEN AS YOU WALK. THE PATH IS EASY TO HEAR.

DON'T TREAT ME LIKE A CHILD! I AM THE ONE WHO CAN SEE! YOU ARE BLIND!

SEE... BLIND? AH, POOR BOGOTÁ. YOUR WORDS HAVE NO MEANING.

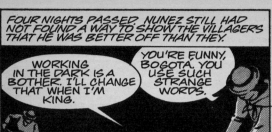

FOUR NIGHTS PASSED. NUNEZ STILL HAD NOT FOUND A WAY TO SHOW THE VILLAGERS THAT HE WAS BETTER OFF THAN THEY.

WORKING IN THE DARK IS A BOTHER. I'LL CHANGE THAT WHEN I'M KING.

YOU'RE FUNNY, BOGOTA. YOU USE SUCH STRANGE WORDS.

TIRED ALREADY, BOGOTA? YOU'VE ONLY JUST STARTED.

HOW... HOW DID YOU KNOW I WAS SLOWING DOWN?

THE SMELL OF YOUR SWEAT WAS BECOMING WEAKER.

HUH! YOU MAY SNIFF LIKE A DOG, IF YOU LIKE. BUT I HAVE THE POWER OF SIGHT!

IF YOU WANT TO STAY WITH US, YOU MUST LEARN TO LIVE AS WE DO, AND FORGET YOUR SO-CALLED "POWERS."

IF I DO WANT TO STAY,... IT IS ONLY FOR THE LOVE OF YOU, MEDINA.

HUSH NOW, BOGOTA. THIS IS NO TIME TO SPEAK OF LOVE. BACK TO WORK.

AT FIRST WARMTH, THE TIRED WORKERS RETURNED TO THE VILLAGE.

MEDINA, YOUR BEAUTY RIVALS THE MOUNTAINS, THE SKY, THE SUNRISE.

WHAT ARE "MOUNTAINS" AND "SKY"? AND WHAT IS "BEAUTY"?

BEYOND THE WALL OF THE VILLAGE, THERE ARE ROCKS PILED UP ON MORE ROCKS. THEY GO UP UNTIL THEY SEEM TO TOUCH THE SKY, WHICH IS MILES ABOVE. AND "BEAUTY" IS THE SMILE ON YOUR FACE.

THERE IS NO WORLD BEYOND THE WALL. AND EVERYONE KNOWS A SMILE WHEN THEY HEAR IT.

BUT I CAN SEE YOUR SMILE. JUST AS I SEE YOUR FATHER ENTERING THE HOUSE WITH A LARGE BASKET. THIS IS THE POWER OF SIGHT.

DID YOUR POWER TELL YOU THAT IN THE BASKET ARE LLAMA STEAKS? DIDN'T YOU HEAR MOTHER SETTING THE TABLE FOR FOUR.?

I...I DIDN'T SMELL THE STEAKS...NOR HEAR THE DISHES.

POOR BOGOTA, YOU'VE SO MUCH TO LEARN. I CAN HELP YOU.

NEXT MORNING, NUNEZ WAS AGAIN TRYING TO EXPLAIN THE GIFT OF SIGHT TO THE VILLAGERS.

THERE'S PEDRO-- TOO FAR OFF TO BE SMELLED OR HEARD!

IN A LITTLE WHILE, PEDRO WILL BE HERE.

BUT PEDRO HAS NO BUSINESS ON THIS PATH.

AS THE OLD MAN SPOKE, PEDRO SUDDENLY TURNED ONTO A DIFFERENT PATH.

SO, WHERE IS PEDRO?

WHAT ELSE CAN YOUR "SIGHT" TELL YOU?

BOGOTÁ-- KING OF IDIOTS!

DON'T INSULT ME! I'LL TEACH YOU THE VALUE OF SIGHT!

NUNEZ HESITATED. THEY STOOD ALERT, AWARE OF HIS THREAT.

I ...I CANNOT HIT A BLIND MAN.

114

FRANTIC, NUNEZ RUSHED THROUGH THEIR LINE.

BUT MORE OF THE VILLAGERS JOINED THE CHASE.

IN TOTAL PANIC, NUNEZ RAN AWAY FROM HIS PURSUERS, ALONG THE WALL THAT CIRCLED THE VILLAGE.

AN OPENING! SAFE!

NONE OF THE VILLAGERS FOLLOWED HIM OUTSIDE. SOBBING AND OUT OF BREATH, HE COLLAPSED.

Phew! SO... MUCH... FOR MY KINGDOM... AMONG THE BLIND!

NUNEZ STAYED OUTSIDE THE VALLEY OF THE BLIND FOR TWO DAYS AND NIGHTS WITHOUT FOOD AND SHELTER.

I MUST GO BACK. I'LL DIE OUT HERE.

HE CRAWLED BACK DOWN TO THE OPENING IN THE WALL. ON THE OTHER SIDE WERE A GROUP OF THE BLIND MEN...WAITING FOR HIM.

LET ME COME BACK, PLEASE! I KNOW I ACTED MAD BEFORE. BUT I WAS ONLY "NEWLY MADE." I AM WISER NOW.

THEN NUNEZ BEGAN TO WEEP, FOR HE WAS VERY WEAK AND ILL FROM THE COLD.

CAN YOU STILL "SEE," BOGOTA?

NO, THE WORD MEANS NOTHING.

AND WHAT IS BEYOND THE ROCKS?

NOTHING AT ALL. IT IS THE END OF THE WORLD.

WE WILL LET YOU BACK. BUT YOU MUST FOLLOW OUR RULES. AND WORK HARDER THAN YOU DID BEFORE.

ANYTHING! ONLY PLEASE LET ME HAVE SOME FOOD, OR I SHALL DIE.

SO NUNEZ BECAME A CITIZEN OF THE COUNTRY OF THE BLIND. HIS SIGHT HAD NOT MADE HIM THEIR KING, BUT IT DID HELP HIM TO FALL IN LOVE.

AGAIN FRESH WATER FOR BOGOTA?

HE WORKS SO HARD, FATHER.

DRINK, NUNEZ. IT WILL KEEP UP YOUR STRENGTH.

YOU CALLED ME NUNEZ! YOU ARE THE ONLY ONE HERE WHO TREATS ME AS A PERSON.

THE MEN AREN'T EVIL--THEY DON'T REALLY WANT TO HURT YOU. IF THEY CALL YOU "IDIOT," IT IS ONLY BECAUSE THEY DON'T KNOW YOU AS I DO.

THANK YOU, MY DEAR. JUST BEING WITH YOU GIVES ME STRENGTH.

IT'S A MISTAKE, MEDINA. IF YOU WANT TO MARRY, THERE ARE PLENTY OF NICE, YOUNG MEN IN THE VILLAGE. BUT, SINCE YOU SAY YOU ARE IN LOVE WITH BOGOTA, I WILL SPEAK TO THE ELDERS.

YES, YACOB. WE AGREE THAT HE IS BETTER THAN HE WAS. SOMEDAY HE'LL BE A FULLY FORMED MAN, AS WE ARE.

THEN... YOU GIVE CONSENT FOR MEDINA TO MARRY HIM?

FIRST, HE MUST BE CURED. THOSE THINGS WHICH HE CALLS "EYES" HAVE AFFECTED HIS BRAIN.

A SIMPLE OPERATION WILL REMOVE THOSE IRRITATING BODIES, AND HIS SUFFERING WILL END.

AND THEN HE WILL BE CURED? THANK GOD FOR SCIENCE!

YACOB WENT TO TELL MEDINA AND NUNEZ THE GOOD NEWS.

NUNEZ GAVE HIS CONSENT. THE DAY BEFORE THE OPERATION, HE TOOK A LAST WALK WITH MEDINA.

IT SHALL HURT BUT LITTLE, MY LOVE. AND IF A WOMAN'S HEART AND LOVE CAN DO IT, I WILL REPAY YOU.

TOMORROW... I SHALL SEE NO MORE.

HE LOOKED AT HER SWEET FACE FOR PERHAPS THE LAST TIME.

YOU SHOULD GO NOW AND PREPARE FOR TOMORROW. GOODBYE, MY LOVE.

BUT NUNEZ DID NOT GO BACK TO HIS HUT.

THE SKY IS BEAUTIFUL TODAY. SEE HOW THE SUN GLINTS OFF THE ICE AND SNOW LIKE A MILLION DIAMONDS! AND HOW LOVELY THE MOUNTAINS ARE!

TOMORROW, MY WORLD WILL END WITH THIS WALL.

AS NUNEZ STARED, HE SPOTTED WHAT SEEMED TO BE A PATH THROUGH A SNOW-COVERED SLOPE. FURTHER UP HE SIGHTED A DISTANT TRAIL.

NUNEZ GLANCED BACK AT THE VILLAGE OF THE BLIND. HE THOUGHT OF MEDINA, BUT ALREADY SHE HAD BECOME SMALL AND REMOTE IN HIS MIND.

BY SUNSET HE HAD CLIMBED HIGH AND FAR.

KNOWING HE MIGHT NOT FIND HIS WAY SAFELY DOWN THE MOUNTAIN, NUNEZ WAS STILL SATISFIED. AS NIGHT DEEPENED HE PEACEFULLY WATCHED THE GLEAMING VEIL OF COLORFUL STARS...

...AND SMILED, AS HE THOUGHT OF HIS ESCAPE FROM THE VILLAGE-- THE PLACE WHERE HE THOUGHT TO BECOME KING!

THE COUNTRY OF THE BLIND
by
H. G. Wells

H. G. Wells can be called the "grandfather" of the fantasy–science fiction tale. Years before this type of story became popular, he was exploring the future in books such as *The Time Machine*, *The War in the Air*, and *The Invisible Man*.

In 1898 he wrote a fantasy called *The War of the Worlds*, which had to do with the invasion of earth by creatures from Mars. Forty years later, Orson Welles dramatized this book in a famous radio program. The drama was so convincing and realistic that all over New England people rushed into the streets with guns and pitchforks, ready to fight the "Martian invaders"!

"The Country of the Blind" tells the incredible story of a land deep in the jungles of South America—a land where only one man has eyes with which to see.

Now that you've read this story, ask yourself:

- The tale is set in a fantastic place. Did Wells make it seem real to you?

- Do you agree or disagree with Nunez's final choice?

- What would you have done if you were in Nunez's place?

THE LEOPARD MAN'S STORY
BY
JACK LONDON

Story Adapted and
Illustrated by Rick Geary

"THIS LION TAMER'S BIG ACT WAS PUTTING HIS HEAD IN A LION'S MOUTH.

"THE MAN WHO HATED HIM ATTENDED EVERY PERFORMANCE, IN HOPES OF SOMEDAY SEEING THE LION CRUNCH DOWN.

"YEARS WENT BY, AND BOTH MEN GREW OLD.

"AND, AT LAST, WHILE SITTING IN THE FRONT ROW, THE MAN GOT WHAT HE WANTED. THE LION CRUNCHED DOWN."

NOW THAT'S WHAT I CALL PATIENCE. IT'S MY OWN STYLE, BUT IT WASN'T THE STYLE OF ANOTHER FELLOW I KNEW.

"HE WAS A FRENCHMAN NAMED DEVILLE... A THIN, LITTLE, SAWED-OFF JUGGLER AND KNIFE-THROWER."

"HE HAD A NICE-LOOKING WIFE WHO DID TRAPEZE WORK HIGH IN THE AIR."

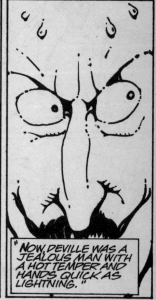

"NOW, DEVILLE WAS A JEALOUS MAN WITH A HOT TEMPER AND HANDS QUICK AS LIGHTNING."

"ONE DAY, THE RINGMASTER MADE THE MISTAKE OF CALLING HIM SEVERAL INSULTING NAMES.

"IN AN INSTANT, DEVILLE HAD PUSHED THE MAN AGAINST HIS KNIFE-THROWING BOARD AND PINNED HIM THERE IN A FLURRY OF DEADLY BLADES.

"FROM THEN ON, WORD WENT AROUND TO WATCH OUT FOR DEVILLE."

"NO ONE DARED BE MORE THAN CIVIL TO HIS WIFE.

"BUT THERE WAS ONE MAN WHO WAS AFRAID OF NOTHING: WALLACE, THE LION TAMER. 'KING' WALLACE, WE CALLED HIM.

"ONCE I SAW WALLACE ENTER THE CAGE OF A MAD LION AND BEAT HIM TO A FINISH WITH JUST A FIST ON THE NOSE.~"

"HIS BEST TRICK WAS ONE OF PUTTING HIS HEAD INTO A LION'S MOUTH."

"FOR THIS HE WOULD ALWAYS USE 'OLD AUGUSTUS,' AN AGING BUT DEPENDABLE BEAST."

"WELL, MADAME DEVILLE BEGAN TO LOOK AT KING WALLACE, AND KING WALLACE BEGAN TO LOOK AT HER."

"DEVILLE LOOKED AT THEM BOTH, AND DIDN'T LIKE WHAT HE SAW."

"I TRIED TO WARN WALLACE... HE JUST LAUGHED AT ME."

"AND HE LAUGHED AT DEVILLE. ONE DAY THE LITTLE FRENCHMAN WANTED TO FIGHT... AND KING WALLACE SHOVED HIS HEAD INTO A BUCKET OF PASTE."

132

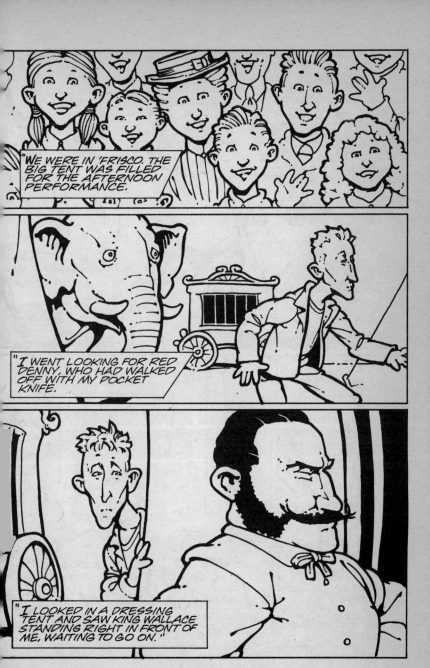

"WE WERE IN 'FRISCO. THE BIG TENT WAS FILLED FOR THE AFTERNOON PERFORMANCE.

"I WENT LOOKING FOR RED DENNY, WHO HAD WALKED OFF WITH MY POCKET KNIFE.

"I LOOKED IN A DRESSING TENT AND SAW KING WALLACE STANDING RIGHT IN FRONT OF ME, WAITING TO GO ON."

"HE WAS HAVING FUN WATCHING A LOUD QUARREL BETWEEN TWO TRAPEZE ARTISTS.

"BUT THEN I SAW DEVILLE, IN ANOTHER CORNER OF THE TENT, STARING AT WALLACE.

"EVERYONE'S ATTENTION WAS ON THE FIGHT... ONLY I SAW WHAT HAPPENED NEXT."

"DEVILLE WITHDREW A HANDKERCHIEF, AS IF TO MOP HIS BROW.

"HE THEN WALKED SLOWLY PAST WALLACE'S BACK.

"AND WITH A FLICK OF THE HANDKERCHIEF, KEPT ON WALKING...

"GLANCING BACK ONCE, A LOOK OF TRIUMPH ON HIS FACE..."

"I WATCHED HIM LEAVE THE CIRCUS GROUNDS AND BOARD AN ELECTRIC CAR.

"MEANWHILE, WALLACE STARTED HIS ACT, HOLDING THE AUDIENCE SPELLBOUND."

"HE WHIPPED 'OLD AUGUSTUS' INTO POSITION.

"AND PUT HIS HEAD BETWEEN THE GAPING JAWS.

"BUT THIS TIME, WITHOUT WARNING, THE OLD CAT CRUNCHED DOWN."

THE LEOPARD MAN'S STORY
by
Jack London

Jack London led a wild and romantic life. Born in 1876, he sold papers and worked on ranches as a boy. After trying college for a while, he tramped around the country and sailed the seas. He also went to Alaska to take part in the Gold Rush in the Klondike.

His most famous novel is *Call of the Wild,* a powerful story of dogs and men. Two of his other famous books, *White Fang* and *The Sea Wolf,* were written at around the same time.

He also wrote short stories that appeared in collections. ''The Leopard Man's Story'' is one of them.

Now that you've read this story, ask yourself:

- Do you think the author really knew a lion-tamer?

- Do you think this is basically a story of revenge?

- Was the ending truly a surprise for you? How did the author create surprise?

THE WATER GHOST OF HARROWBY HALL

BY
JOHN K. BANGS

Story Adapted by Fred Schiller

Illustrated by Sterling Brown

THE PLACE: HARROWBY HALL--A MODEST HOTEL, JUST SOUTH OF LONDON.

THE TIME: 11:59 P.M. CHRISTMAS EVE, 1986.

NOW WHERE DID I PACK MY TOOTHBRUSH? OH, DEAR... EVERYTHING'S GOTTEN SO... SO...

...DAMP!!

141

THE NEXT MORNING...

HE WARNED ME... JUST BEFORE HE DIED, POPPA WARNED ME.

...NEVER RENT THIS ROOM ON CHRISTMAS EVE, HE SAID... ALWAYS KEEP PLENTY OF UMBRELLAS AROUND, HE SAID. NOW I UNDERSTAND.

BUT POPPA'S GONE, AND I'M IN CHARGE NOW... AND NO WATER GHOST IS GOING TO GET THE BETTER OF ME.

WE'LL JUST SEE HOW THE WATER GHOST OF HARROWBY HALL LIKES DEALING WITH HENRY HARTWICK OGLETHORPE!

143

CHRISTMAS EVE, 1987. MIDNIGHT.

IT BEGINS WITH A LIGHT MIST...

...BUT IN THE SPACE OF A HEARTBEAT, BECOMES A DOWNPOUR.

THE FOOLISH NEW OWNER BELIEVES ME SO EASILY DEFEATED ? HE SHALL LEARN...

HE SHALL LEARN REGRET... FEAR...HORROR!

NO GHOST IS GOING TO GET THE BETTER OF ME!

145

"MY FATHER, HUSTON HARROWBY, BUILT HARROWBY HALL. THE ROOM THAT I HAUNT WAS TO HAVE BEEN MINE.

"FATHER TREATED ME LIKE THE SON THAT HE NEVER HAD.

"IT WASN'T MY FAULT THAT I'D BEEN BORN A GIRL INSTEAD OF A BOY.

"MY NEW BEDROOM WAS FURNISHED AS ONLY A BOY COULD LIKE... HE DID IT TO SPITE ME.

"HE TOLD ME THAT IF I DIDN'T LIKE IT THAT WAY, THAT I COULD SLEEP ON THE LAWN.

"LATER THAT NIGHT... CHRISTMAS EVE 1787... I RAN FROM THE HALL IN TEARS, HAVING DECIDED TO TAKE MY LIFE."

"I JUMPED FROM THE CLIFFS INTO THE SEA.

"BUT ALTHOUGH I DIED, I DID NOT PERISH. A FULL WEEK PASSED BEFORE I LEARNED WHY.

"A SEA NYMPH CAME TO ME, AND EXPLAINED THAT I WAS NOW ONE OF HER FOLLOWERS.

"BECAUSE OF THE MANNER OF MY DEATH, I MUST RETURN TO HARROWBY HALL FOR AN HOUR, EVERY CHRISTMAS EVE... AND HAUNT WHOEVER IS IN MY ROOM, OR THE CURRENT OWNER OF THE HALL."

HOWEVER, HENRY NEVER HAD THE CHANCE TO PLOT HIS REVENGE.

THE SOAKING FROM THE WATER GHOST THAT NIGHT LEFT HENRY WITH A BAD FEVER...

...FROM WHICH HE NEVER RECOVERED.

HENRY HARDWICK
R I P
A GOOD MAN SWEET MAN

HENRY LEFT ALL THAT HE OWNED, INCLUDING THE HOTEL, TO HIS NEPHEW NIGEL--

WILL

--A BRIGHT YOUNG BUSINESSMAN, WHO WAS NOT ABOUT TO BE OUT-SMARTED BY A GHOST --OF ALL THINGS.

SHORTLY BEFORE HIS DEATH, HIS UNCLE HENRY HAD WRITTEN OF HIS MEETING WITH THE WATER GHOST IN HIS DIARY.

NIGEL STUDIED THE DIARY FOR DAYS.

UNTIL, AT LAST, HE HAD FOUND THE ANSWER.

SNAP!

153

154

CHRISTMAS EVE...
MIDNIGHT...1989.

NIGEL FELDMAN...

ARE YOU MAD, OR JUST A FOOL?

NEITHER, I JUST WANT TO STAY WARM.

BUT THIS INN IS WELL HEATED!

BUT WE'RE GOING OUTSIDE-- WHERE IT'S BELOW ZERO!

155

156

THE WAREHOUSE'S FROZEN UNIT IS THE FINEST IN THE COUNTRY.

FELDMAN FROZEN FOOD WAREHOUSE

ENTER ⬇

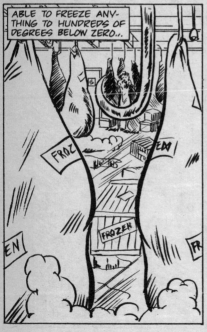

ABLE TO FREEZE ANYTHING TO HUNDREDS OF DEGREES BELOW ZERO...

INCLUDING PESKY WATER GHOSTS.

THE WATER GHOST OF HARROWBY HALL

by

John K. Bangs

John K. Bangs lived and worked in New York City. He was a writer and an editor. For a while he edited the magazine *Harper's Monthly*. Later, he worked for *Life*, which was then a humor magazine.

As an author, Bangs turned out plays, poetry, children's books, and short stories. Most of his ghost stories have a funny twist. Among his books are *Toppleton's Client* and a collection called *The Water Ghost and Others,* from which this story is taken.

In "The Water Ghost of Harrowby Hall," Bangs manages to turn the story of an unhappy ghost into a humorous tale.

Now that you've read this story, ask yourself:

- What gave this strange phantom her watery image?

- Bangs has played it for laughs. But how could you take the same plot and make it scary?

- Which do you enjoy more—ghosts who are scary, or ghosts who are funny?

*S*UBWAY
BY
THE EDITORS

Story Adapted
and Illustrated by Rick Geary

"MY FAMILY AND I HAD JUST MOVED TO NEW YORK CITY, AND IT WAS MY FIRST DAY OF SCHOOL. I HAD NEVER FELT SO SCARED AND ALONE."

WHAT A BIG, STRANGE PLACE.

"WORST OF ALL, I HAD TO TAKE THE SUBWAY. I'D NEVER SET FOOT ON ONE IN MY LIFE."

TIME TO LEAVE, DONNA. REMEMBER TO BE CAREFUL ON THE SUBWAY.

I WILL, MOM.

162

163

164

165

167

168

SUBWAY

by
The Editors

After reading through hundreds of "creepy tales" to choose the contents of this book, we decided to try writing one ourselves. "Subway" was written and adapted to comics by the editors and one of our favorite artists, Rick Geary.

This is a story about a familiar city experience. Now that you've read it, ask yourself:

- Do you remember your first time on the subway?

- Do you think the girl's mother over-reacted or "told it like it is?" Explain.

- Have you ever had an experience where you misread what was happening, as this girl did? What actually happened?

THE WIND IN THE ROSEBUSH
BY
MARY WILKINS FREEMAN

Story Adapted by Fred Schiller

Illustrated by Frederic Lere

MORNING! YOUR FIRST VISIT TO FORD VILLAGE, MISS?

YES, IT IS. I HAVE TO LOCATE A MRS. EMELINE DENT -- MY LATE BROTHER'S WIDOW. DO YOU KNOW HER?

UMM... YOU'RE KIN TO EMELINE DENT? HAVE YOU EVER MET HER?

NO, THIS IS MY FIRST VISIT FROM MICHIGAN. I'VE COME TO BRING MY NIECE, AGNES, BACK WITH ME. SHE IS MY BROTHER'S DAUGHTER FROM HIS FIRST MARRIAGE -- AND IS NO BLOOD TO EMELINE DENT. DO YOU KNOW AGNES?

WE, UMM... NO -- WE DON'T.

WE SHOULD HAVE TOLD HER.

TOLD HER WHAT? NO ONE KNOWS WHAT REALLY HAPPENED UP AT THAT HOUSE. SHE'D BEST FIND OUT FOR HERSELF.

172

WELL, I'LL SOON BE THERE! I WONDER IF AGNES STILL LOOKS LIKE HER OLD PHOTO. I HAVEN'T SEEN A NEW ONE IN YEARS.

I HOPE HER STEPMOTHER HAS TAKEN GOOD CARE OF HER. BEFORE HE DIED, JOHN USED TO WRITE THAT THE TWO DIDN'T GET ON WELL.

SO SHE SHOULDN'T MIND ME BRINGING AGNES BACK TO MICHIGAN.

HERE WE ARE, MA'AM.

EMELINE DENT? I'M REBECCA, JOHN'S SISTER. I WROTE YOU THAT I WAS COMING FOR AGNES.

YES...YOU'RE SOONER THAN I EXPECTED.

174

175

YOU HAVE A BEAUTIFUL HOME, MRS. DENT. I SEE MY BROTHER PROVIDED VERY WELL FOR YOU.

YES, BUT I HAD MONEY ENOUGH OF MY OWN, AS WELL.

YOU HAVE TO BE THRIFTY IN THIS WORLD, OR YOU'LL WIND UP PENNILESS IN YOUR OLD AGE. YOU REMEMBER THAT.

YES, MA'AM, I WILL. WHAT TIME DID YOU SAY MY NIECE WOULD BE HOME?

GOODNESS! IT'S ALMOST TIME FOR TEA!

176

177

178

REBECCA WAITED UP LATE FOR AGNES. EMELINE DENT LATER RECALLED THAT THE GIRLS HAD A SCHOOL SOCIAL TO GO TO.

SHE KEEPS SUGGESTING THAT I CATCH THE NEXT FERRY AND RETURN TO MICHIGAN—THAT SHE'LL SEND AGNES ALONG IN A FEW DAYS.

THERE IS SOMETHING ODD ABOUT THIS HOUSE. I'LL BE GLAD TO TAKE AGNES AWAY FROM HERE.

GOOD MORNING, EMELINE. DOESN'T AGNES HELP YOU WITH THE BREAKFAST CHORES?

WELL, YES, BUT...

...BUT SHE'S NOT HERE. SHE MUST HAVE SPENT THE NIGHT OVER AT ADDIE'S.

WITHOUT SENDING WORD? DIDN'T SHE KNOW THAT WOULD WORRY YOU?

AGNES IS A BIG GIRL--NEARLY SIX-TEEN. SHE CAN TAKE CARE OF HERSELF.

181

LATER THAT AFTERNOON...

HOW WAS YOUR NAP? AGNES SENT WORD THAT SHE'LL BE STAYING WITH ADDIE SLOCUM FOR A FEW DAYS.

WHAT? BUT SHE KNOWS THAT I'M HERE FOR HER, DOESN'T SHE?

WELL, YOU KNOW HOW CHILDREN CAN BE. WHY DON'T YOU GO HOME, BACK TO MICHIGAN— AND I'LL SEND AGNES UP IN A FEW DAYS.

NO! I'M NOT LEAVING FORD VILLAGE WITHOUT HER!

I'LL GO TO THIS ADDIE SLOCUM AND BRING HER BACK MYSELF!

THIS IS THE ONLY HOUSE FOR MILES--THIS HAS TO BE IT.

AT LAST, I'LL SEE AGNES!

WHY... THERE'S NO ONE HERE. IT ALMOST LOOKS DESERTED.!

...AND IT LOOKS AS IF THE HOUSE HAS BEEN CLOSED UP. I DON'T UNDERSTAND.

THEY MUST HAVE PACKED UP AND GONE AWAY FOR A FEW DAYS.

DON'T WORRY... THE SLOCUMS WILL TAKE CARE OF AGNES.

OH, I'M SO TIRED...AND I'M AFRAID I'M NOT FEELING WELL AT ALL. I'M GOING TO LIE DOWN AWHILE. CALL ME IF YOU HEAR ANYTHING, WILL YOU?

WHAT'S THE MEANING OF THIS? EMELINE? MIZ DENT!

185

THAT CAME EARLY THIS MORNING. I SEE IT'S FROM MICHIGAN.

YES, IT'S FROM MY COUSIN -- WHO'S BEEN LOOKING AFTER MY HOUSE WHILE I'M HERE. SHE SAYS ALL IS WELL, AND THAT A FRIEND HAS COME TO STAY WITH HER.

BUT WAIT... MY COUSIN'S FRIEND HAS ADDED A NOTE. SHE SAYS THAT MY COUSIN FELL DOWN AND BROKE HER HIP, AND SHE NEEDS MY HELP.

WELL, YOU HAD BETTER GO, MY DEAR, AND LOOK AFTER YOUR KIN. WHEN AGNES GETS BACK I'LL SEE TO PACKING HER UP AND SENDING HER TO YOU.

REBECCA HAD LITTLE CHOICE. BUT SHE LEFT FORD VILLAGE FEELING UNEASY.

WHEN SHE REACHED HOME, REBECCA'S SUSPICIONS PROVED CORRECT. HER COUSIN WAS IN PERFECT HEALTH, AND HER FRIEND HADN'T WRITTEN THE POSTSCRIPT ONTO HER LETTER.

IT'S CLEAR TO ME NOW-- EMELINE DENT DID THIS. I MUST RETURN TO FORD VILLAGE, TO FACE HER.

BUT HER RECENT TRAVELS AND WORRIES HAD TAKEN THEIR TOLL. REBECCA BECAME ILL.

NEVERTHELESS, REBECCA WAS STILL WORRIED ABOUT AGNES AND THE EVENTS IN FORD VILLAGE. SHE WROTE TO THE POSTMASTER THERE. ALL HER QUESTIONS WERE ANSWERED IN HIS REPLY.

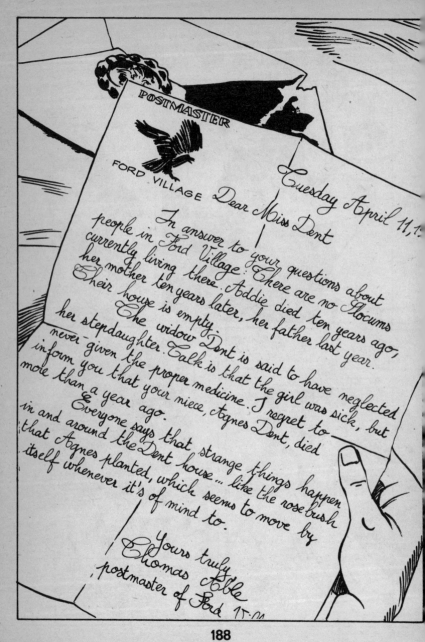

POSTMASTER

FORD VILLAGE

Tuesday April 11, 1...

Dear Miss Dent

In answer to your questions about people in Ford Village: There are no Slocums currently living there. Addie died ten years ago, her mother ten years later, her father last year. Their house is empty.

The widow Dent is said to have neglected her stepdaughter. Talk is that the girl was sick, but never given the proper medicine. I regret to inform you that your niece, Agnes Dent, died more than a year ago.

Everyone says that strange things happen in and around the Dent house... like the rose bush that Agnes planted, which seems to move by itself whenever it's of mind to.

Yours truly
Thomas Able
postmaster of Ford V...

188

THE WIND IN THE ROSEBUSH
by
Mary Wilkins Freeman

Mary Wilkins Freeman was born in 1852. She was a frail, little girl who couldn't go to school. However, this did not stop her from doing a good deal of reading. She educated herself and went on to become secretary to the famous jurist Oliver Wendell Holmes. Mary Wilkins was a close observer of other people and she was very good at portraying small-town life. Two of her best-known works are *A Humble Romance* and *A New England Nun and Other Stories*. During her lifetime Mary Wilkins Freeman wrote 238 short stories, twelve novels, a play, and two volumes of verse. *The Wind in the Rosebush* was written in 1903.

This story depends on creating a mood. Now that you've read this story, ask yourself:

- How does the author give you a feeling of impending mystery?

- Do you find the plot believable? Why or why not?

- Could something like this have happened today? Why or why not?

About the Editors

SEYMOUR V. REIT, Senior Associate Editor of the Bank Street Media Group, is author of over fifty books for children, and several non-fiction books for adults. He is also a cartoonist, and the creator of "Casper the Friendly Ghost."

BARBARA BRENNER is a writer, teacher and editor. She has written over forty books for children. Mrs. Brenner is a Senior Associate Editor with the Bank Street Media Group. She is married to illustrator Fred Brenner.

HOWARD ZIMMERMAN, a former public school teacher, is Special Projects Editor for Byron Preiss Visual Publications, Inc. He has created and edited several magazines for kids, including "Comics Scene," and has written several books on science fiction.

Share the Adventure and the Excitement of

The Bank Street Collection

Pocket Books and Bank Street, America's most trusted name in childhood education, introduce THE BANK STREET COLLECTIONS of Science Fiction, Fantasy, Creepy Tales and Mystery—graphic story comics from some of America's best cartoonists and authors.

THE BANK STREET BOOK OF SCIENCE FICTION
63145/$3.95
Authors include Andre Norton, Damon Knight, and Isaac Asimov.

THE BANK STREET BOOK OF FANTASY
63146/$3.95
Authors include H. G. Wells, Anne McCaffrey and Terry and Carol Carr.

THE BANK STREET BOOK OF CREEPY TALES
63147/$3.95
Authors include Edgar Allan Poe, and O. Henry.

THE BANK STREET BOOK OF MYSTERY
63148/$3.95
Authors include Bret Harte, Dashiell Hammett and Isaac Asimov.

Simon & Schuster Mail Order Dept. BST
200 Old Tappan Rd., Tappan, N.J. 07675

Please send me the books I have checked above. I am enclosing $_____(please add 75¢ to cover postage and handling for each order. N.Y.S. and N.Y.C. residents please add appropriate sales tax). Send check or money order—no cash or C.O.D.'s please. Allow up to six weeks for delivery. For purchases over $10.00 you may use VISA: card number, expiration date and customer signature must be included.

Name_____

Address_____

City_____ State/Zip_____

VISA Card No._____ Exp. Date_____

Signature_____